To those who need a reminder to
just keep breathing:

You are loved.
You are valuable.
You can do hard things.

For Mental Health help
Call or text
988
Suicide and Crisis Lifeline

SISKO

Just keep breathing
I beg of her
She is the stronger one
The younger one
The smarter one
The reckless one
The one who lives forever
The vivacious one
She's alive
So full of life
Just keep breathing
Just
Keep
Breathing

At times I felt I hated her
For pestering me
For her hateful words
For the scars I carried on my body
Because of her
She was a baby, though
My little doll
My responsibility
My little "sisko"
And for her
I would have moved the world

Daddy turned mommy around
Holding her up from the ground
My ballerina
They laughed and kissed
Before he gently put her down

This place is daunting and cold
It's far too clean
The machines are deafening
Don't unplug them, though
I'll keep the whirring
And the beeping
Of these machines
I fluff her pillows
And tuck her tighter
In the too white sheets

The
Quietness
Is
Killing
Me

She and I walked through
A field of overgrown weeds
The smell of honeysuckle surrounded us
Watch out for snakes
Our grandpa breathed
The world is cruel for ruining summer days
And good walking weeds
With snakes

She steals my clothes
And damn her for being
Taller
Skinnier
Prettier
Because they all look better
On her

She was sick
And bit the thermometer
When Mama checked for a fever
The mercury danced in her belly
Like little worms she said
Auntie was scared
Because mercury was dangerous
I would have thought it would have been the glass
I was terrified
And they rushed her away
Leaving me behind with auntie and crying
But now we all laugh
About the little worms dancing

Just keep breathing
I brush and braid her hair
I stain her lips with a neutral colour
She'd hate for these doctors
To see her
Without her precious makeup
Just keep breathing
I tell myself
To keep my hands from shaking
I fill in her eyebrows
Two perfectly angled dark twins
I laugh
Because I always compared them
To the Evil Queen's
Just keep breathing
And help me, please
You know I'm no good
At this makeup thing
I'm not good at many things
You are the one who is better
At everything
And I need you
To just keep breathing

She was terrified of dogs
Which was odd
Because I had been bitten
Not her

I think I preferred the machines
When they were making their
Noises
And obnoxious beeps
I was wrong
The quietness is
What is truly deafening

She called me
Screaming on my voicemail
Her car had broken down
But it was my night shift
At the diner
And I didn't have time
To save her

I vividly remember the shots
I took
And the cheap beer
In the ridiculously small
Fraternity house
Which wasn't really a fraternity house
I didn't even like the taste
Back then
But I drank them
Long necks down

She was drinking, too
Just across town
If only I knew then
What I know now

RAKKOUS

Have you grown weary of me
Or are you imagining you are protecting me
With your absence
Did I love you too much
Did I over pry
Was I not pretty enough for you
Did you find someone new
Please come back
I promise
I'll be better for you
I'll be just enough
Nothing too much

In Finnish "Rakkous"
Means love
In Finnish "Rikki"
Means broken
They are so similar
In my mind
They are the same
If you cannot love so deeply
That you are broken
When it's gone
Surely then
You did not love at all
And the words
They intermingle
And intertwine
And crash into each other
This broken love of mine

There she is
My girl
He whispers in my ear
As he stands behind me in the mirror
Wrapping his arms around my waist
Resting his chin on my shoulder
And his cheek against my face
He makes me blush
And smile
When we are alone
How dare he
Control my expressions
For a split second
I see beauty in my reflection

I have grown to hate the scenery
Because he is not here
Pick a mountain, I'll tell him
I'll pack my bags
And meet him there
We can fall completely off the grid
Build our own cabin
Live from the land
I would want for nothing
No new scenery
Once I'm there
There with him
Anywhere with him

RIKKI

He kissed me deeply
With his fingers wrapped in my hair
And his breath filled my lungs
Each time I inhaled
Let someone come along
And kiss me better

My
Body
Aches
From
Thinking
Of
Him

No.
Fuck you.
You do not get to
Simply
Disappear.

RAKKOUS

He compliments me
In my messy morning hair
And stupidly believes
I look best in my sweats
I smile always
Like the fool I am
For loving a man
As wild and free as him

Of course
I miss you
It's all
I ever do

I cannot emphasize enough
How he has been
With all the wrong people
And I cannot stress all the ways
I would be perfect for him
But I just sit and listen
He sits and talks
Just out of my grasp
As he talks about all of the
Imperfect ones
And how love isn't real
It never lasts

He holds me together
When my world caves in
I'm tired of people, I say
He says, well, fuck them

I speak his name so casually
In conversation
As if everyone I speak to knows
I tell strangers about him
They look in my eyes
And immediately
They think I'm in love

If he would just
Come home
I'd make him the blackest coffee
In the French press I desperately wanted
And all the pasta
He could dream
If he would just come home
To me
But he is wild and free
And home is a "silly made up construct
Of things"

He loved that stupid old red truck
Something was always broken
And he was always fixing
Maybe that's why he couldn't
Stay for me
He could only try to fix
One broken thing

Why would he leave me
When I need him
I keep having nightmares
Only to wake up
Catching my breath
Sweating and panicking
Reaching out for him like I once did
But of course
He isn't there

She's so sick

I realise I've been holding my breath
And finally, I breathe
I cry into his arms
I haven't said these words out loud
And I let them slip out
I melt into him
His muscular body
Folds around me like pillows
She'll be okay
Is all he can say
And I breathe in his scent
Of cigars and whiskey

How was she today

I know he'd rather
Talk about coffee
Or soccer
Or the weather
Or anything else
Not so serious
I know he'd rather me be strong
Not see me like this
This brokenness
But he asks anyway
And gives me a gentle kiss
Today was a good day for her
I say, then force a smile
And pour us both a drink

The night we met
He grinned at me
After I downed my second
Or maybe my third drink
I like tall girls
Who can handle their whiskey

SISKO

She called me
Crying on my voicemail
But I was frozen in my fear
I didn't know
How to save her
I could never
Save her

The first time
Her body betrayed her
I thought she was drunk
I thought she was foolish
For drinking so much
Stumbling around
Nearly passing out
But I had to catch her
From falling face first on the ground
And there was no smell
Of any alcohol to be found

I thought it more than ridiculous
That doctors couldn't
Tell us what was wrong
There was something wrong
Run another test, anything
What are they waiting for
What the hell
Had they gone to school for

She has expensive taste
Everything she does is a show
So it's no surprise to me
That she's taking her sweet time
To wake up
Because that will be
The grandest and most exquisite thing
She has ever done

VISKI

The flame quickly licked my fingertips
But I still held the wooden match stick
Let it burn, I thought
Burn like the bridge
I looked across the ravine
Deep and daunting
The smell of smoke filled the air
And I realised
Once again
I had forgotten to breathe
I waited there for an eternity
Waited to see if he had come after me

It's all coming back to me
In nightmares
I don't want to see

I leaned over
And put my head on his shoulder
He grabbed my hand
To shift the gears with him
It was so hard to shift
The gears with him
So I gave up
And sighed
I breathed him in
And closed my eyes

He always smelled
Of some cologne
And a good hint of
Cheap cigars and whiskey
It was my
Favourite smell

I wore my red lipstick
He hated it
But I loved to kiss him
And leave lip prints
Here try one
I pressed my red lips against it
And he lit the cigar
A long drag and
He smiled that smile
I choked of course
I'll stick to whiskey
I decided
And took a swig from the half-empty bottle

He walked into my life
At just the perfect time
Perfect eyes
Perfect jawline
Perfect hair
Perfect smile
Everything else was chaos
But him in his perfection
He'd just pour me
Another round

SISKO

We dated brothers one time
That was a tragic mess
But it was our little secret
Sisters best kept

He said to tell you hello
Oh how the hell is the old boy
When is he ever going to show his face around
In time, sis, I told her
You'll meet him in time

I held her hand
And prayed
God I don't care what comes out
Just let me hear her sailor's mouth

I told him all about you
Did you tell him I'm the pretty one
No. I'm hoping he thinks that's me
Let me a see a picture of him
I can't, sisko, we haven't taken any

When she was younger
She had this incredibly soft
Little Mermaid blanket
She could not sleep
Or function
Or seemingly breathe
Without

MURTAA

I don't know the cocktail
He mixed for me tonight
But I'm praying
It's
A
Strong
One

I led him to the cabin
Secluded in the woods
I'm very tired
I told him
But he wouldn't carry me

He wiped
My tears
I was shattered
Out of my trance
How long
Had I been crying

Let's go out tonight
I begged
I'll fix my hair
And wear a dress
And paint my lips red
Let's stay in instead
He pulled me deeper in the bed

SISKO

Just

Keep

Breathing...

I pray by her bedside
That she would walk again
I know God will
Just breathe into her
With His divine breath
He did it for Adam, and then for Eve
He can do it for her
He can just reach down and breathe
And she will wake up
From this drug out nightmare
I just know God
Will show up
And she will not just breathe
But she'll get up

Daddy held mommy
Holding her up
From collapsing to the ground
My baby
Was all she could manage
And he kissed her
Before gently easing her down

MURTAA

My scream pierced
The deafest ears
And I found myself on the ground
My body was disfigured
Not even a fetal position
Could keep me safe
He picked me up
Where have YOU been
I growled and spat at him
I was waiting, love
For you to come around
Let's take a drive
I've got the truck running
I'll let you shift the gears
Your hand on mine
It was hard to shift the gears
That night
I leaned over to him
Gave up
And closed my eyes

VISKI

The sirens and lights
Startled me
And punctured a throbbing pain
Through my eyes and deep into my head
I must have fallen asleep
What the hell happened
Where were we
My eyes were heavy
It was hard to breathe
Where did he go
I tore at my seatbelt
And fought open the door
I tried to stand
But the lights and sirens
Knocked me back
Confusing me
Where is HE
I think I screamed
But my mouth was dry
And the sirens stifled me
I tried scanning the wooded area
Searching for a trace of his body
One glimpse of his perfect body
Not one blood mark
In the old red truck
He must have gotten free...

Ma'am...it's time to go
They lifted me and strapped me down
Lift on 1..2..3...
And I felt myself leave the ground
They ushered me away
The heat from the fire rushed over me
The truck
The red truck
He adores so much
Nothing but flames
They didn't even look for him
In the wreckage
No.
Fuck you.
You do not get to
Simply
Leave him.

There were
Red lip prints
On my hand
From when I tested my lipstick
And hair entangled in my fingers
When did I lose
This much hair

Black dress
Black tights
Black shoes
Black mascara running from my eyes
I forgot how
To wipe my own tears
Red lips
Red eyes
Heavy arms hanging by my sides

I wore my red lipstick
I hated it
But I loved to remember him
And imagined his lips pressed against mine
I lit the cigar
And laughed
I never choked anymore
I took another long drag
And flicked the ashes
In the empty bottle on the floor

His kisses tasted like
Cinnamon
Baby
He was a fireball

RAKKOUS

He slipped a simple silver ring
On my left hand
As we lay next to each other
In my unkempt bed
Everything with him
Was simple
And I loved every simple moment
The simple perfection

I woke up
And could still smell him
Cigars and whiskey
But he'd not been in my bed

SISKO

Mama just sat down
Beside me
After she figured out
That I'd been crying
She needs her
Mermaid blanket, Mama
I had been searching
Mama had no words for once
And squeezed my hand
She needed her blanket to rest
To heal
To function
To breathe
Even though I knew
That blanket had been gone
For an eternity

SURU

Hi,
My name is Mercy
I stare at the unblinking faces
In the circle
I'm assuming they all know
But they wait until I say the rest
And I'm here
Because I lost someone
I love
I mean
I loved...
When someone dies
Verbs become past tense
And I digress myself from rambling
The unblinking faces respond to me

Hi, Mercy

Tell us a little about
The person
Try to remember
Something good

Everything about him was good
How can I choose just one moment
One memory
He kept me
From losing my mind
Out loud I tell her
He always smelled like
Cigars and whiskey
Cheap cigars and cheap whiskey
I suppose that memory will have to suffice
The lady writes skeptically
Behind her hidden clipboard
She doesn't believe
They didn't search for him
She pushes me to remember more
Something else
But I never can
She keeps knocking on a bolt locked door

Clipboard lady
I'm sure she has a name
But I never bother with such things
She always seems afraid of me
Like I was going to explode
I was not the one to fear
If you asked me
I would've checked the lady's purse
Who had the purple hair

I spilled my coffee
On my favourite gown
I should have gotten it
In black

SISKO

We would play Barbie dolls
But they'd never be in love
Or playing house
There would always be
A competition
A comparison
That was our lives
A race to win
And usually
She did

She was the more
Athletic one
It never made sense
Why her body was the one
That betrayed her

I have scars on my arms
From our fights as children
They look magnified in this light
I count them
While she's sleeping and silent

Wake up, sisko
I whisper
I dare you to try and fight

DON'T MESS WITH THE BEST
I would cheer her on
From a roaring crowd
People tried to defend her
But she'd give them hell
Ace
Dig
Spike
She's going places fast
Leaving this small town

2 AM texts
About
The ~~man~~ boy
Who hurt her
I should have killed him
For her
But I could never save her

How many times
Did we have to watch
Her favourite movie
Mama and I hid the DVD
I couldn't take another
repeat

SURU

Hey Mama
I kiss her cheek
And welcome her in
She rarely visits
Because she's busy
Taking care of sister
She sits uncomfortably
On my couch
And looks at my night clothes
She hates when
I don't change out of my gown

She tries to talk about the weather
About celebrities
About small town people
About everything
Except
What happened to me
It's okay Mama
I'm fine, I tell her
A tear rolls down her cheek
She checks the time
Kisses me goodbye
Don't forget to drink your water
And eat
And tells me
She has to leave
She didn't even stay
To finish her tea

Daddy calls to check on me
The old land line rings
Religiously
I'll see you soon
He chokes a bit
Getting out the words
Our calls are short
Simple and sweet
He was never one
For many words

Pouring coffee is my job
I do it better than anyone, really
And I hide all the creamers
And the sugars
So people have to drink it
Black
The way it was meant to be

MURTAA

I slammed the coffee cup
Against the wall
The ceramic shattered
And the coffee splattered
I liked the way it felt
So I threw them all

I dipped the brush
In the chemicals
And let the fumes fill my lungs
I painted my hair
Like Van Gogh would have
Thick brush strokes
Heavy on the paint
Changing the golden blonde
To black
The way it was meant to be
I slipped the scissors from the kitchen drawer
Like Milo sculpting
I started chopping
At the curls
A masterpiece

SISKO

DON'T MESS WITH THE BEST
I would beg to God
From a too quiet hospital room
People tried to pull me away
But I'd give them hell
Just
KEEP
BREATHING
I was going nowhere
Never leaving her in that town

Look what I've got
It's your favourite movie
I found it hidden at Mama's house
I bet I still know every word
Wake up
We can watch it on repeat together

We were left alone
Daddy was at work
Mama just had to run
To the store
We were so little
But old enough to be left alone
And I didn't know
That asthma
Could make a face turn so blue
So quickly

RAKKOUS

He led me down to the water
So we could go
Fishin' in the dark
He carried the poles and bait
And I carried the bottles
He flashed the light
Through the weeds
And onto the lake
I thought I'd caught a fish
But not that night
How cruel the world is
To ruin a perfect fishing night
With snakes

He held me up
And spun me around
My love, he called me
He made me dizzy
When we spun
Round and round
Pour me another
Round and round
Everything about him
Was perfect
But he made me so dizzy
This was the only
Not simple thing

He loved the thunder
Thunder meant
No one could hear
If we were loud
Our clumsy bodies stumbled
Fumbled
Crashing into the bed
The wall
The floor
I loved his kisses
He loved to hear the
Thunder roar

You're such a child
He teased me as I
Made myself into a burrito
In my
Little mermaid blanket
I couldn't remember
Why I loved it so much

No.
Fuck you, September
For taking
My love
And not
Me

SURU

Hi, Mercy
Clipboard lady
Asks how I take my coffee
Before she gets settled
In her chair
To ask about my nightmares
The contradiction of warmth
In her yellow cardigan
When she asks about the things
That haunt me
Very seriously
That's how I take my coffee
I can't help but smile
He always said that
It was the only thing
He was ever serious about

There it was
The nightmare
The shaking
The inability to breathe
It'd been a few days
But I knew it'd return
The one of the old red truck
Slamming into the tree

Mercy, let's try this one more time
Do you know why I'm here to help you
Because I lost someone I love
I mean, I loved
Can you tell me how you lost them
One more time, please
I'd just left from visiting my sister
We were in the truck
And had a wreck
Can you tell me more about your sister
She was very sick
She's much better now
I hear myself say the words
But they do not sound right
Something is not right

MURTAA

Why do YOU look
So damn sad
I finally snap
Clipboard lady was there
To help me grieve my love
Or supposedly that was her job
I ripped the clipboard from her hand
What the hell is THIS
There were notes of course
Of everything I had ever said
And a paragraph of bold typed words
That read
FAMILY HISTORY
PARENTS: MARRIED
MOTHER: ALIVE AND WELL
FATHER: ALIVE AND WELL
SISTER: DECEASED, SEPTEMBER 18
DIAGNOSIS: PSYCHOSIS
DATE OF ADMISSION: SEPTEMBER 24
SEE ACCIDENT REPORT

Mercy, honey
You were alone that night
That's your truck
You'd had a lot to drink
And were pretty messed up
There was no body to be found
Mercy…
Honey…
There was nobody
I feel something inside me break
I am suddenly aware I am wearing
A paper gown

The world is cruel
For one cannot walk through life
Without fear
Of deception
When the snake
Is one's own mind

See: Accident Report
Date: September 24
Name: Mary E. Adler, 19
Other party(s): none
Officer notes:
Highly intoxicated
Open containers of whiskey
Smell of cigars
No indication of other drugs
Disoriented female driver
Red truck
Single vehicle collision
High rate of speed
Lost control
Crashed into tree
No passengers
Truck totaled in fire
Hysteria
Recommended: inpatient psychiatric evaluation

In Finnish "Murtaa"
Means break
In Finnish "Muuttaa"
Means change
They are so similar
In my mind
They are the same
If you are living a life
In which you never break
You will never experience
Change

MUUTTAA

I've patiently counted to thirty now
I glance above her brightly coloured head
And see my prized expensive paper
MD, doctor of medicine
With a specialty in psychiatry
And of all people
Awarded to me
I try to introduce myself again
Because she's somewhere else and didn't hear me
Hi, my name is Dr. Adler
But you can call me Mercy

I stare at her unblinking face
As her eyes watch the ceiling fan circle
I tap the clipboard gently with my pen
To get her attention from the fan
Hi, Mercy
My name is Audrey
Tell me a little about yourself
Try to tell me
Something good

This is heavy but I am accustomed to
People with weighted thoughts
Needing weighted blankets to ground them
From the clouds
I am accustomed to absent-minded gazes
And people who cannot quite grasp the traumas
Their grey mattered brain
Won't let them face, yet

Let's start from the beginning
I nudge her to recall events
Tell me things about the person you lost

Stop your tapping
I don't need another person behind a clipboard, lady
Pushing me
I'm not crazy...
Tell her, Johnny, I'm not crazy
Audrey, who are you talking to
Johnny, he's standing to the left of you
He knows you're writing things about me
What the hell have you been writing about me
She attempts to snatch the clipboard from
My hands
And I give it up graciously
Hallucinations?
Nightmares?
PTSD?
I'm NOT crazy...

Close your eyes
Take deep breaths in
Find a place in your mind that is peaceful
And makes sense

I know you're not crazy, Audrey
But you have experienced trauma
Just keep breathing
Let's start from the beginning

I met Johnny two years ago
I was dancing in the crowd
And he was sitting at the bar
He walked so confidently up to me
And grabbed my hand and spun me around
Spun me so fast
He had to hold me up
From falling to the ground
I'm Johnny, he smiled
We laughed and he leaned in and kissed me
And baby, it was magic

I vividly remember the fight
We had
And the way my mascara dripped
From my eyes
And across my hands as I tried
To wipe them dry
As I screamed at him
But he couldn't hear me
Because it was raining
And he drove away in that stupid truck
He had been drinking, too
And if only I know then
What I know now
...I still don't know what I would do

I wonder if she saw my eyes shift
When she mentioned a stupid truck
These things are heavy
But I am accustomed to heavy lifting
I have been doing this for quite some time now
She speaks his name so casually
In conversation
As if she knows I simply know about him
I see it in her eyes
Immediately I know she was in love

I am reminded of a time where
I would attempt to fix my old red truck
Grandpa first showed me how when I could barely
See over the hood
And he'd say
Watch out for your fingers
Don't let them get in the way
Don't let yourself get in the way
His hands and mine dirty from the grease
And lessons on summer days

Something was always broken
And I was always fixing
Maybe that's why I couldn't fix myself
I could only fix one broken thing

The world is cruel
For taking grandpas away
Before I could learn how to fix
Everything

She called me
Screaming on my voicemail
Dr. Adler...
Mercy...
I can't breathe
I think I've cut myself too deep

I tried to call her back immediately

The ringing is deafening
Please
Answer
Me

How was she today
I know
That he's not supposed to know
About the patients that I see
But I talk about her
Over coffee
Or the weather
Or anything else
And he is a partner and cares about my
Serious things
And he cares about her
Because he cares about me
She is a special case
I want to break her free
From this brokenness
And he asks anyway
And gives me a gentle kiss
Today was a good day for her
I give him a hopeful smile
And he pours us both a cup of tea

The day we met
Her eyes were sunken and grey
And although he was gone
She kept talking to Johnny
Who was always standing behind me
Always out of her grasp
Just too far away
Always out of her reach
And I asked her about him
And she kept saying
I'm not crazy
Tell her Johnny
I'm not crazy
But tears escaped and trickled down her cheeks
Ask johnny to sit down with you
I offered once, but he won't
He wants to see what you're writing
I want to see what you're writing
While you hide behind your clipboard, lady
You're not crazy, Audrey
But you are hurting
And I want to help you
I think it's ridiculous
That you're a doctor and you can't
Tell me what is wrong
What the hell did you go to school for

It all came back to me
In nightmares I had forgotten
I'd seen

I stayed with her, my sisko
As her breath left her body
I prayed beside her hospital bed
Just open your eyes
I dare you to wake up and fight
And then the plug was pulled
And the machines slowly stopped their whirring
The silence was deafening
But what came next was worse
They call it
The death rattle
Where lungs give way
And the air inside them shakes
And the body stops working
But it's not just one moment
It's a thousand minutes waiting
And they give medicine to ease
The gurgling sounds
And doctors and nurses
Hang their heads down
Oh, the silence
It takes its sweet time
And it is the most incredible thing
To hold someone's hand when they
Stop breathing
To suddenly have to speak of someone
In the past tense
Because for a fleeting moment they were
Here on this earth
And there are never enough moments
And the next moment
They cease to exist
A shell of my sister, my sisko
She had expensive taste
And everything she did was a show
So it is no surprise to me
That she took her sweet time dying

Her life was
The grandest and most
Exquisite thing

I lean over and put my head
On his shoulder
He grabs my hand
To ease the remote away from me
It is hard to make decisions
When everything feels so heavy
So I give up
And sigh
I breathe him in
And close my eyes

I, ironically
Or maybe symbolically
Wore red lipstick
The day I left the facility
My mother told everyone
I went on vacation
And we never talked about it again

I was studying at the coffee shop
Later than they'd like
But they never complained
And I'd tip them extra
I just didn't know how to study at home
And one day the door opened
Are you guys still open
I noticed the sign is still on
The lights are still on

He caught a glimpse of me
Before I saw him
But when I did, and our eyes met
The flame quickly lit inside of me
I didn't know there were any matches left
I didn't know there was light still inside me
And I realised
I had forgotten this whole encounter
That I wasn't breathing
I waited an eternity
And waved my hand to the chair next to me
If you don't mind the chaos
You can study with me
And when he tells the story
This is where my eyes shone up at him
And he fell in love instantly

I'm Jonah
Hi, my name is Mercy

He walked into my life
At the most imperfect time
Kind eyes
Soft jawline
Tussled hair
Crooked smile
Everything was chaos
But him in his softness
He kept coming back to the coffee shop
He said he came for the coffee
But he stayed for me
He said
He liked tall girls
Who drank black coffee

I visit Audrey
She sits uncomfortably on her bed
And she doesn't notice that she
Has coffee stains on her paper scrubs
I ask the nurse to get her fresh ones
The light is always too bright
And makes depressed faces
Glow dauntingly
I internally count to thirty patiently
I have scars on my arms, too
I was not expecting to say this out loud
And ethically this is not what I should do
But something draws me to her
And I think she feels it too
They look magnified in this light
I have them and there are five hundred thirty-two
Five hundred thirty-two times I wanted to feel
Something different than emptiness
And five hundred thirty-two times I gave in
To feel pain
Instead of whatever else was surrounding me
And those do not count the times I wanted to die
Because that was too many times to put a number to
She looks at me quizzically
And I think for the first time
Actually sees me

He's gone...isn't he, Mercy?

There it was
The grey matter caught up
The dam broke
Her scream pierced
My ears
And I found myself on the ground
Her body was disfigured
Not even a fetal position
Could protect her now
I scooped her up
She wailed
And cried
And punched the floor
She clutched the neck of her paper scrubs
I can't breathe, Mercy
And she found that paper scrubs are easily torn
It was heavy for her to keep fighting
And she leaned over
And gave up crying
And closed her eyes
Let me wrap her in my arms

I saw our reflection
And I held that girl
A reflection of myself
Where I once laid on that floor
I told that girl
And I told myself
It's not okay
It wasn't okay
And I know you're hurting
But hold on, child
Healing is coming

Sisko	Sister
Viski	Whiskey
Murtaa	Break
Suru	Grief
Rikki	Broken
Rakkous	Love
Muuttaa	Change

Made in United States
Orlando, FL
29 March 2024